Bella

Rebecca Barber

Book Boyfriend Publishing Pty Ltd

This is a work of fiction. Names, characters, organizations, places, events, and incidents are either products of the author's imagination or are used fictitiously. Any resemblance to actual events, locales, or persons living or dead are entirely coincidental.

© Rebecca Barber. ALL RIGHTS RESERVED

No part of this book may be reproduced, or stored in a retrieval system, or transmitted in any form or by any means electronic, mechanical, photocopying, recording, or otherwise, without express written permission of the publisher.

This book is licensed for your personal enjoyment only. This book may not be re-sold or given away to other people.

Published by Book Boyfriend Publishing Pty Ltd.

Cover Design by: KatDeezigns

Editing by: More Than Words Editing

Proofreading: M Neal

Contents

Dedication	IV
1. Bella	1
2. Matteo	6
3. Bella	14
4. Matteo	23
5. Bella	30
6. Matteo	37
7. Bella	40
What Next?	43
Also By	45
Acknowledgements	48
About the Author	50
Stay Connected	51

Dedication

To everyone everywhere who believes in love

Chapter One

Bella

I couldn't believe I was doing this.

That I was really here.

Venice had been on my bucket list forever, and finally here I was, standing in the middle of St. Mark's Square, surrounded by people and pigeons unable to wipe the smile from my face.

Rubbing my belly protectively, I adjusted my sunglasses and headed for my hotel. The sooner I checked in and dumped my bags, the sooner I could get out and explore. I only had five days to see everything before returning home to Canada, and I was planning on making each moment count.

Three wrong turns later, and I was lost.

Shoving my suitcase against the wall, I balanced my butt on the top of it and pulled out my phone, searching for directions. Yep, I was walking in the wrong direction. Normally something I'd be frustrated by, but I was in Venice. I couldn't be anything other than overwhelmed with awe. Less than two hours in the city and I was already in love.

Backtracking the way I came, I dragged my suitcase over the cobblestone paths ignoring the burn in my arm as my case bounced back and forth while my purse hung over my shoulder slapping me in the stomach with every step.

As I rounded the corner, I ran straight into the strong muscular body of a man who towered over me. I was five-seven, and this guy had a good six inches on me. With scruff on his jaw and piercing blue eyes, eyes so blue they rivaled the sky, I felt my body flush with heat, something I'd never experienced before.

"*Scusate*," he said in a deep voice with a thick Italian accent.

I didn't speak the language but knew enough to make me dangerous. Besides lasagna and cappuccino, I could get around, but there was no way I'd be able to hold a conversation without making a fool of myself.

With no words, I forced a smile and shook my head. His scent so deep and masculine was sending me crazy and making this smart girl dumb, it was enough to make me forget my name, and when he smiled at me, deep dimples popping, I almost fainted. I wanted to blame the lack of food and sleep, I'd barely slept a wink on the flight over, but I knew it was the man in the navy suit, with the expensive gold watch wrapped around his wrist, and mischief in his eyes that was responsible.

Stepping to the side, I let him pass, and when his phone rang it shocked us both out of the trance we were locked in. Answering it, he replied quickly in Italian causing my panties to flood. Whoever said Spanish was the language of love had obviously never heard a man like this speak Italian.

Frozen where I was, I watched him go, and when he looked back over his shoulder and winked, it took everything I had not to race after him. Taking a deep breath, I pushed aside all thoughts of the beautiful businessman and headed to my hotel. After that I needed a cold shower and a change of underwear.

After checking into Hotel Monaco and Grand Canal, I made my way up to my room. A room with a view worth paying for. If this was my last hurrah before I settled down, then I was making the most of it, splurging for a suite with a view from the bed of the Grand Canal.

Dropping my purse on the bed, I threw open the windows and took in the beauty before me. Everything was exactly as I dreamt of. The gondolas on the canals. The architecture. It was so much better than the pictures, and I couldn't wait to get amongst it. But first, food. My stomach rumbled loudly, and I guess there was an upside to traveling alone. Only this time I wasn't really alone. At least I was hoping I wasn't. I wouldn't really know until I got home, but I had everything crossed that this round of IVF had worked and this was my babymoon.

Stripping off, I stepped into the overly opulent bathroom and turned on the faucet. I'd never seen so much gold in one room. Everything was inlaid with gold. The tiles on the walls, the light fitting, and even the taps were gold. It was completely over the top and I loved it.

A quick shower and change later and I was sliding my feet into my sandals, pushing my hat on my head, grabbing my room key, and heading back out the door. For the past six weeks, from the moment I'd booked my flight, I'd started researching and planning. If it was a once in a lifetime experience, then I was going all in.

Heading back to St. Mark's Square, this time without my suitcase, I went slowly, taking my time to look in the windows of the stores, in awe of the beauty I found there. When I came across a store window filled with delicate, beautiful glass objects, I was lured inside by their intricate design and vibrant colors.

"*Ciao*," the older gentleman behind the counter greeted me with a warm smile. He looked like my grandpa I remembered so well and missed so much. With a head full of thinning white hair, he wore a button-down shirt and dark pants with suspenders holding them up over his thickening belly. But it was the look on his face that made me miss Grandpa even more. Something about the softness in his eyes invited me in.

"Ciao," I replied back emotionally.

"*Inglese?*"

"Si, grazie," I tried, my accent terrible.

"Ah. Very good, bella. American, si?"

Panic wrapped around me. How did he know my name? Come to think of it, the desk clerk at the hotel had called me Bella too, but I hadn't thought anything of it. Ignoring the weird feeling, I answered politely.

"Canadian."

"Ah. Very good. Please, look around."

"Grazie," I replied, moving away from him toward the display cases full of the intricate artworks.

They were beautiful. Vases and bowls. Jewelry and frames. Even candlestick holders. They were all so stunning I wished I could take them all home. But my bank account and my luggage limit weren't going to make that possible, so instead, I bought myself the most gorgeous bracelet I'd ever seen. It was burnt orange and red and so completely unique I couldn't walk away without it. Made from delicate Murano glass, it would look perfect with my black dress, and I couldn't wait to put it on.

Quickly I paid for my purchase, dropped the box in my purse, and headed back out into the piazza, focused on finding something to eat. It was too early for dinner, but I was starving and couldn't wait. Besides, there was a very good chance I was eating for two. A thought that made me smile.

Ducking into the first restaurant I found, a quaint little place right on the piazza, I was immediately seated. With white linen tablecloths, low light, and raucous laughter, I ordered a mineral water while checking out the menu. Ten minutes later and the only decision I'd made was that I wanted it all. Pizza, pasta, bruschetta, and even the seafood sounded too good to go past.

The waiter appeared, a young man with a terrible excuse for growing a mustache but perfectly pressed pants and a crisp white shirt. After topping up my glass, he took my order and left me sitting there admiring my surroundings. This place was amazing with a bar along the side made of heavy timber with sparkling glasses hanging above.

While I was daydreaming about what tomorrow might bring, that was after I climbed the Campanile all ninety-six meters of it, a man caught my eye as he breezed through the doors, confidence and charisma oozing from him. When he flashed a beaming white smile I almost fainted. I'd recognize those dimples anywhere. And I certainly wouldn't forget them. The same man who knocked me off my senses and buckled my knees was striding through the restaurant, shaking hands with the staff and greeting them warmly. When his eyes met mine, I wished the glass in my hand was filled with something stronger than mineral water.

Chapter Two

Matteo

S he was here.

The angel who nearly knocked me on my ass, my fault, I was running late to a meeting and wasn't watching where I was going, but she was here. Out of all the restaurants in Venice, she chose my uncle's to stop into tonight. And to think I wasn't going to come by. I'd planned on heading straight home to change before hitting the gym, but instead I'd chosen a whiskey and a bowl of Uncle Giovanni's gnocchi. I'd run off the pasta tomorrow, but seeing her sitting there had me forgetting about my shitty afternoon.

After ordering my drink, I strode straight over to her table, watching as her eyes widened as I approached. I had an effect on this girl. No doubt about it. The way her cheeks turned pink, the way her breath came in perfect little pants causing her tits to rise and fall, and what spectacular tits they were. She'd changed since I'd run into her in the alley. Before she'd been wearing a pair of jeans that molded to her curvy ass perfectly with a thin white top that she might've believed wasn't see-through, but I swear I could recount in perfect detail every scrap of lace that held those big, beautiful boobs captive. I was a loud and proud tits and ass man, and this woman had the perfect amount.

"Ciao," I greeted as I came to a stop beside her table.

When I'd run into her earlier, she'd been silent not saying a word, and all afternoon as I listened to my CFO drone on and on about profit and loss and being risk-averse, she was all I could think about. I wanted to know if her voice was as sweet as her face. I wanted to know if she tasted as good as she smelt. I wanted to know it all.

"Hi," she squeaked quietly, looking around the room.

"Mind if I join you?" I asked, switching to her native tongue, trying to put her at ease.

"S-sure," she replied, although she didn't sound convincing. Not that I was going to let that stop me. I hadn't gotten to where I was playing it safe, something that was a bugbear of my entire executive team, but I was the boss so they could get over it.

Reaching across the table, I took her hand, her left hand, double-checking for a ring before leaning down and kissing the soft skin. Damn, she smelt amazing. My dick was already straining my pants and I had to reach down and adjust myself, desperate to find some extra room.

"I'm Matteo," I introduced myself.

"Bella," she replied so sweetly.

"A beautiful name for a beautiful woman."

I watched as her cheeks darkened at my compliment. "And where are you from, Bella?" I asked, trying to keep the conversation light and not blurt out every thought I was having.

"Canada."

"Ah. The country that's filled with moose and snow."

"We have other things!" she protested, and it was so damn adorable. Sweeping her off her feet was getting harder and harder to resist.

When our waiter, a young, nervous guy set her plate down in front of her, almost spilling it in her lap, I shot him a look that had him recoiling and my uncle darting over to smooth over the situation. Giovanni knew me well. He knew I wasn't a patient man and incompetence wasn't tolerated. In my business, time meant money and money was something not to be squandered. I'd grown up with none, and now that I had more than I could ever need, I wasn't about to throw it away over some bratty little kid who couldn't pay attention.

"Matteo," my uncle warned.

"Giovanni. Meet Bella. Bella, my uncle, Giovanni."

Even though he was my own family, when he bent down and kissed Bella's hand, just as I had done, a weird surge of jealousy raced through me. Something I hadn't felt before and something that caught me off guard. I'd just met Bella. She lived in another country, one half a world away, yet she was mine. I already knew it. I felt it. Now all I had to do was convince her.

"Nice to meet you." Bella smiled up at my uncle with a tenderness that didn't help the situation.

But Giovanni knew me, probably better than I knew myself. That's why the asshole prolonged my agony, showering Bella with compliments and answering all her questions. Why she was so chatty with him when I could barely get two words out of her was frustrating yet intriguing. She was a puzzle, one I was desperate to unravel.

"Enjoy your meal, Bella. And if you need anything, please just ask," Giovanni added before disappearing into the kitchen, not before throwing a wink in my direction and hiding if he knew what was good for him.

BELLA

Bella picked up her fork before looking over at me. I was content to sit there and watch her eat. She was effortlessly stunning, and I'd been with my fair share of beautiful women, but somehow Bella put them all to shame.

"Please," I gestured toward her plate.

She took a teeny bite. There's no way she could've even tasted it, it was that small.

"Bella, please start. Mine will be here momentarily."

"But you haven't even ordered," she retorted just as the jittery waiter appeared with my dinner, the same bowl of gnocchi Bella had ordered. "Oh."

"I have the same thing every time," I offered as a way of explanation, picking up my fork and taking a bite.

Slowly, Bella followed suit, and soon enough, we were eating normally and chatting away about nothing in particular. She told me about her dream to see Venice and all that it entailed. I'd lived here most of my life and had come to despise how touristy it had become. As a businessman, I understood the attraction of the tourist dollar, but seeing how low people would stoop to get it made me sick to my stomach. But I couldn't tell her that. In fact, I had a better idea.

"What are you doing tomorrow, Bella?" I asked, catching her off-guard.

"I...I...just a second."

After wiping her mouth with a napkin, not that she needed to, she was perfect just the way she was, Bella dug her phone from her purse and looked something up.

"Tomorrow I am going to go to see the Bridge of Sighs, ride in a gondola, eat lasagna, check out Museo Correr, and Museo del Risorgimento..."

I grinned. I couldn't help it. Hearing her attempt to say their names was gorgeous. Even though she stumbled over the pronunciation, I couldn't bring myself to correct her.

"What? Did I say that wrong?" Bella asked as embarrassment tinged her cheeks.

"You're doing perfectly. What else is on the list?"

"And then I thought I'd end the day having coffee at Historic Cafe on Piazza San Marco."

"That's a big day," I commented.

"It is. But I'm only here for a few days. I have to make the most of them."

"And let me guess, you've got each one scheduled out on your phone there?"

Bella looked away. I'd nailed it. "What if I offered you a better suggestion?"

"Depends on the suggestion. Like I said, I've only got a few days."

"Well then, better make it count. Let me show you Venice," I offered before I had a chance to think it through.

"I couldn't ask you to do that, Matteo," Bella dismissed, but hearing my name fall from her lips was enough to have me canceling everything to spend every second I could with this enchanting woman. I don't know what it was about her, but I was desperate to know it all. A realization that should terrify me, but instead made me cling even tighter to the idea.

"You're not asking me to, Bella. I'm offering."

"I'm sure you're too busy…" she protested, and she was right. I was too busy. I had board meetings, takeover meetings, and a million and one other things to do, but right now, none of that mattered. Nothing did except making this beautiful woman smile.

"Never too busy for you."

BELLA

"Will you take me on a gondola?" she asked, stars in her eyes.

"Absolutely," I promised, pushing aside my hatred for the things. If that's what Bella wanted, then she was going to get the full experience. Our Gondolier was going to wear the striped shirt, hat and sing as he navigated through the canals making this beautiful woman's dreams come true.

"If you're sure I'm not taking you away from anything."

"Nothing that can't wait."

Clapping her hands together, Bella bounced in her seat, her tits bouncing with her, captivating my eyes. "I'm excited," she squealed.

"Me too, Bella. Me too."

And the sad truth was, I couldn't remember the last time I'd been excited, not to mention the last time I'd taken a day off. This was going to be fun. I was looking forward to it.

We finished up dinner and Bella went to pay, but Giovanni refused to take her money. "Anyone who can make my grumpy Matteo here smile gets a free meal," he joked.

Instead of pocketing her cash, Bella shoved her money into the tip jar and thanked Giovanni for his hospitality and the delicious meal before stepping out into the dying sunlight.

"Can I walk you back to your hotel?" I offered, not ready to say goodnight just yet.

"Actually, I'm not going back yet. I'm off to climb..."

"Ah. The Campanile."

"Would you like to join me?" Bella offered nervously.

"I'd love to, Bella, but another time perhaps. I need to make some arrangements for tomorrow for us."

"Please don't go to any trouble."

Bella had no idea the extent of the trouble I would go to for her. If she wanted to see Venice, then I would give her an authentic experience. She would come to love this place as I did and perhaps, maybe she'd consider staying a little longer.

"It's no trouble, Bella. Trust me," I invited, fascinated when she crooked her head to the side before a smile swept across her face.

She stepped toward me and pushed up on her toes, holding onto my shoulder for balance. When she pressed her lips to my cheek, I felt my heart pound, threatening to break through my chest.

"Thank you for dinner, Matteo. It was nice to have company."

"You're welcome, Bella."

"I'll see you tomorrow morning?" she said, making it sound like a question.

"I'll pick you up at your hotel at nine."

"Perfect," she replied, and I had to bite my tongue to stop myself from replying, 'yes, you are.' "Have a good night, Matteo."

"Buonanotte angelo mio."

"What does that mean?"

"It means good night, my angel," I answered her honestly.

Bella blushed and my work here was done. "Go. You don't want to miss the sunset from the top."

"Oh."

Another kiss on my cheek and my dick was as hard as steel as she slipped away. I stood there like a fool, hands buried in my pockets as I watched the sway of her hips and the bounce of her ass as she crossed the piazza before disappearing amongst the throng of tourists.

My father, God rest his soul, told me the first time he ever saw my mama, he knew she was the one. He'd been working on a ladder, painting some rich lady's home, when Mama walked by with some friends. Papa said he almost fell off, landing on the concrete trying to get to the woman who stole his heart with barely a look. I hadn't believed his story. Love at first sight wasn't real. At least I hadn't thought it was until now. Now, Bella McIntosh from a small town in Canada had me second-guessing everything I thought I knew.

With calls to make and a mountain of things to rearrange, I headed back to the office to take care of business.

Chapter Three

Bella

I was giddy.

I'd been up since six and after two coffees, the best coffees I'd ever had mind you, I was buzzing. Even though I told Matteo I'd meet him at the hotel, I couldn't sit still, so I snuck out early down to the piazza and watched the world go by, trying to kill time while I wondered what he had planned. I had no doubt I'd see more of Venice with him than I would following my guidebook, and spending time with the man who'd haunted my dreams wasn't a hardship either. Keeping my hormones in check on the other hand, that I was going to struggle with.

After changing my clothes twice, unable to decide, I finally settled on a pair of khaki shorts and long sleeve navy top with a white tank underneath, topping it off with a pair of navy walking shoes. If I was sightseeing, then I wanted to be able to do it properly and my experience with the cobblestone paths yesterday meant my heels were staying in my bag.

With one last look out the window at the Grand Canal, something that was more beautiful in person than any photo could ever do justice, I grabbed my bag and headed downstairs to wait for Matteo.

He didn't keep me waiting long. Striding through the lobby like he owned the place, his effect on my body was not normal. He was still more than ten meters away, and my body was responding. Damn hormones. I was blaming the vials of them they'd pumped me full of while I went through the IVF treatment for my reaction.

"Buongiorno, amore mio," Matteo said as he came to a stop in front of me, kissing my cheek softly, and giving me a whiff of his cologne which had me almost swooning at his feet.

"Good morning?" I asked, not quite understanding his comment.

"Buongiorno, amore mio, is good morning, my love," he explained.

"Oh."

What was I supposed to say to that? I'd run into him less than twenty-four hours ago, literally run into him and here he was calling me, my love. Italian men, I sighed. He was going to make it very hard to go home again.

"Are you ready to go? We can stop and get coffee..."

"I've already had two," I admitted, earning me a megawatt smile.

"Well then, let's do it. We have a big day ahead of us, starting with...you'll see," Matteo teased with a wink before taking my hand, lacing his fingers with mine, and ushering me out of the hotel.

If I thought the man was stunning in a suit, seeing him casually dressed was something else. With his own khaki shorts, he wore a white polo shirt which showed off every impressive inch of his muscular body. A body I was so up close and personal with, I could feel the warmth from his skin radiating off me.

Waiting out the front was something I wasn't expecting. A bright red scooter. When Matteo walked over and picked up the helmet sitting on the seat, I almost fainted. Riding around Italy on a scooter was more than I could've asked for. It was one of the things I'd had on my list but dismissed. I wasn't brave enough to try it on my own, especially now when I was being more cautious than ever, but there it was.

"This is yours?" I asked as Matteo brushed the hair from my eyes and slid the helmet on my head before securing the buckle.

"It is. And today, it's ours," he smiled before pulling on his own helmet.

A minute later, with my arms wound around his waist and my head resting against his back we were whizzing through the streets, the sound of our laughter mixing together. I was enjoying the journey so much that when he rolled to a stop I almost groaned, not recognizing where we were.

"*Palazzo Ducale,* Bella," Matteo said, his accent accentuated.

"Can we go in?" I asked hopefully.

"*Sì.*"

As quick as I could, I unbuckled my helmet and attempted to fix my hair. Five minutes in a helmet and I already looked like a mess. When Matteo reached for my hand again, something that was beginning to feel almost too natural, I gave up and instead focused on the incredible building in front of me.

Matteo handed over our tickets, and I looked up at him quizzically. When had he gotten those? With a dismissive shake of his head, he led me inside and instantly all thoughts were forgotten. With its ornate ceilings, paneled rooms, and exquisite artwork, it was like being transported back in time. I didn't know where to look first. It was all so beautiful.

"It's amazing, isn't it?" he whispered into my ear, the warmth of his breath causing goosebumps to break out across my skin.

"How can something almost a thousand years old still look like this?" I asked without expecting an answer.

Matteo stepped in front of me, cupping my face in his hands. "When we Italians love something, we take care of it." His words sounded like a promise. A dangerous promise I could easily convince myself meant more.

Before I could reply, we were moving again.

By the time we returned to the hotel, my feet were aching, my belly was full, and my mind was whirling. It'd been the most incredible day. Matteo had shown me everything I wanted to see and so much more. We toured museums, walked through the Bridge of Sighs, and ate gelato in the piazza. We laughed and exchanged stories. I learned that Matteo was the CEO of his own multimillion-dollar company, and he was playing hooky to spend the day with me.

"You can't do that," I admonished, peering over the cup of my strawberry gelato that was enough to satisfy even the strongest sweet tooth.

"Bella, I'm the boss. I can do what I want."

"But for me..."

"It's worth it."

The way he said it caused my heart to flutter.

Instead of arguing, I let it go—for now. Tomorrow I'd find my own way. It wouldn't be as much fun, and I'm sure I'd miss things, but I couldn't ask him to waste two days out of his office for me. That wouldn't be fair.

Pulling up outside the hotel, Matteo helped me off.

"I want to take you to dinner, Bella."

"Matteo." I sighed. "You don't have to do that. You've already done so much."

"I want to. Please. I'll pick you up at six?"

How could I say no to that? The way his piercing blue eyes looked at me drew the word from my lips before I had a chance to protest.

"Okay," I murmured as a bright smile lit up Matteo's gorgeous face making him look like he'd just won the lottery.

"*Perfetta!*" he exclaimed excitedly, almost as though he expected me to put up more of an argument. Silly man. Even I wasn't dumb enough to turn down a man who looked like Matteo when he offered to take you out for dinner. I might be inexperienced, but I wasn't an idiot.

When he kissed my lips so quickly I thought I imagined it and promised to see me soon, leaving me standing in the lobby, trying to remember the feel of his lips against mine, I knew I was in big trouble. I watched him go through the heavy glass doors and when he tore away recklessly on the same scooter he'd so carefully navigated through the streets all day, I held my breath.

The big ornate clock on the wall above the reception counter chimed, and I realized it was already four in the afternoon. Time had flown, and now I only had two hours before Matteo was back to pick me up for dinner. Snapping out of my Matteo-fueled lust haze, I darted upstairs and started the bath.

By five o'clock I was panicking.

After lying in the bath for half an hour, I'd exfoliated, shaved, and moisturized every inch of my body. Mentally calculating the time difference, I rang my bestie back in Canada hoping she could talk me off the ledge.

"Come on! Pick up. Pick up." I chanted down the line waiting for Violet to answer. "Come on!" I snapped this time more forcefully.

"And good morning to you too, Bella," Violet replied, and I could just picture the smirk on her face. "Oh wait, it's afternoon there isn't it?"

"Hi, Vi. Yeah, it's almost five here."

"How is it? Tell me everything. Is it everything you hoped it would be? More? Have you ridden in the gondola yet? I haven't seen any photos?" Vi gushed out.

Damn, I loved that girl. There was a reason she was my bestie and the only person who knew what was going on in my life. I'd been too scared to tell my parents I was starting a family on my own. They wouldn't understand. Mom would tell me to wait, and Dad would worry. And my brother Wyatt, he'd probably lose his shit completely. They loved me and as much as Mom was crying out for grandkids, being a single mom wasn't what they wanted for me.

"No, I haven't been in a gondola yet. Yes, it's amazing. Yes, it's beautiful. And it's more than I could've ever hoped for."

"Then why the hell are you calling me? We can talk about it when you're back. Or do you miss me already? Oh, that's sweet." Vi giggled to herself.

"Vi! I need your help."

"Oh, shit. Is it the baby?" Immediately gone was the fun, teasing version of my best friend replaced by the caring, compassionate nurse version.

"It's fine. I'm fine. Full of damn hormones that are making me crazy, but that's not why I'm calling."

"Geez, Bella. You scared the life out of me. I've had everything crossed this works for you. I've already been thinking of cool things I can do with my niece or nephew."

And that's why Vi was family. My kid may not have a father in the picture, but there was no doubt they would be loved. When I'd told

Vi I wanted to do this, she hadn't told me I was being ridiculous, she'd just sat down with me and patiently planned it out. We'd weighed up the pros and cons, and in the end, the decision was all mine, and I couldn't walk away. I was a thirty-two-year-old virgin who'd never really even kissed a guy. I didn't have time to wait for Mr. Right to make his appearance to make me a mom. I was a smart, determined, and independent woman. I could do this on my own. So that's what I was going to do.

"Vi! Focus."

This call was probably costing me a million dollars, and it'd be worth every cent if only I could get Vi to focus for a second and listen.

"What's up?"

"I met someone," I stated as silence fell across the line. After what felt like forever when Vi didn't say anything, I asked if she was still there.

"Yeah, I'm here. Just processing. When you say you met someone..."

"Matteo."

"Matteo? Nice name."

"Vi, he's amazing."

"You've only been there for twenty-four hours."

"I know." I couldn't stop smiling.

"Well, what's he like?"

I spent five minutes gushing over the man I'd spent the day with, telling Vi everything I'd learned. He was tall, gorgeous, generous, kind, and smelt wickedly good.

"And you're having dinner with him tonight?"

"Yeah. He's picking me up in...shit!"

"What's wrong?"

BELLA

"Forty-five minutes. He's picking me up in forty-five minutes, and I'm a mess."

"Okay. Calm down. Take a breath. There's plenty of time to make you date ready."

"Date ready? It's not a date, it's just dinner."

"Bella. It's a date."

"Fuck me I need a drink," I exclaimed, sitting on the edge of the most uncomfortable sofa I'd ever sat on. With its teal velvet cushions and gold trim, it might look good, but it was horrible to sit on.

"Well, you might be pregnant so let's skip the wine for now. You can have one glass at dinner."

"Vi?"

"Yeah?"

"I can't do this," I exhaled, disappointment filling my body.

"Why the hell not?" she asked sharply.

"I might be pregnant."

"So? Pregnant women date all the time."

"Pregnant with someone else's baby?"

"Bella, look at it this way," Vi started, sounding like she had some serious wisdom to share. "You're in Italy for four more days. Go. Date. Kiss. Bring him back to your hotel and have wild hot monkey sex if you want. Then come back home and enjoy the memory. It's not like anything can come of it. He lives in Italy. You live in Canada. Almost five thousand miles apart. Enjoy this week for what it is, then come home and tell me all about it."

"You really think I can do that?"

"Protect your heart, Bella, and you can do anything."

I thought about what she said, and it made sense. At least on the surface it did. I wasn't convinced I'd be able to keep my heart out of it, but having fun with Matteo was something I wasn't ready to rule out.

Finally, I replied, "Okay."

"Okay?"

"Yeah, okay."

"Great! Now, let's get you dressed. We need something that's going to bring Matteo to his knees and make him never want to let you go," Vi squealed excitedly not realizing how hard her words hit.

Pushing the what-ifs aside, I got ready for my night out. I was here to enjoy myself, and if that meant indulging a little, then nothing was off the table.

Chapter Four

Matteo

H oly mother of Mary.

I'd already jerked off twice since I'd dropped Bella back at her hotel, but obviously it wasn't enough.

Seeing her standing in the lobby, long, smooth legs on display under a positively sinful red dress was enough to have my dick standing to attention. With her back to me, she didn't see me approach which gave me time to unashamedly ogle her. Her dress cinched around her waist but flared out over her hips while her long mane of dark brown hair, hair the color of the most indulgent chocolate hung in waves around her shoulders.

"*Bellissima, Bella*," I crooned as I got closer, my mother's words echoing in my head.

My mother had found out I'd skipped out on work today, thanks to my nosy assistant's inability to cover, and showed up quite unexpectedly at my apartment demanding to know if I was sick. When I'd told her I'd met someone she practically ripped my grandmother's diamond ring from her finger and forced it into my hand. My *madre* had been at me for some time to give her some grandbabies she could fuss over, but I'd always been too busy with work, which wasn't entirely a lie, so even the hint that there could be a woman in the picture was enough to have her handing over the family heirloom.

When I explained Bella was Canadian and wouldn't be staying in Venice beyond the end of the week, she muttered something in hurried Italian, a string of insults most of which I missed, but I managed to hear her call me a *stupido ragazzo,* a stupid boy.

Now standing here in the lobby, staring at Bella who looked like everything I ever wanted, I had to admit, my mother wasn't wrong. Falling for Bella would be stupid, but I had a feeling I couldn't stop myself even if I wanted to.

She spun around on her three-inch heels, heels that made her already impressive legs look even more delectable. The red dress, a color that I'd been seriously underrating until now, had a plunging deep V in the front, showing only the smallest hint of cleavage. Somehow Bella had managed to pull off classy and sexy in the same dress. Yet it was the wide smile on her face, how kissable her shiny red lips looked that had me ready to go and ask my mother for the ring, long-distance be damned.

"Wow!" Bella exclaimed as I took her hand and kissed it tenderly, unable to keep my hands off her.

"Are you ready?"

"Is this okay? I wasn't sure where we were going or what we were doing. I can go and change..." she started to ramble, and it was adorable, but I needed to cut her off.

"You're *sensazionale,* Bella. Perfect."

She stood a little taller at my compliment and if that's all it took to put that pink in her cheeks, then I would be dishing them out all night.

Taking her arm in mine, I led her out the door to my waiting car. Opening the door for her, Bella slipped into the back seat before sliding over so I could follow. Catching my driver's eye, I nodded, and without a word we were off.

"Matteo," Bella said so softly it made my dick throb. I could just imagine her lying across my chest, her heart still pounding, her naked body covered in a thin sheen of sweat, whispering my name just like that after I'd spent hours drawing every ounce of pleasure from her sexy body.

"*Sì, amore mio?*"

"Where are you taking me?" Bella asked, and I felt her eyes crawl over my body, taking me in. When her breath hitched, I knew I wasn't the only one affected.

"You'll see," I promised with a wink, pulling her across the seat until she was leaning up against me, my arm wrapped around her shoulder, her head buried in the crook of my neck.

Fuck I was in trouble. Everything about this woman pressed my buttons. From her vanilla-scented perfume to the soft waves of her hair tickling my neck, to the flash of creamy thigh I caught a glimpse of as she straightened her dress. How I was going to keep my hands to myself I had no idea. Not to mention keeping my dick in check.

When we pulled up to a nondescript building, Bella looked at me confused. "Trust me," I told her before climbing out of the car, offering her my hand.

Once she was out and steady on those heels I was envisioning digging into my ass as I plowed into her, I led her around the corner onto the dock where our ride was waiting.

"Matteo!" Bella squealed in delight, forgetting herself and throwing herself into my arms, hugging me tightly.

I almost burst.

I almost bust a nut with her curvy body pressed against mine, but my heart also exploded as well. I'd never felt like this before, so in awe, so caught up in someone. Usually, I wanted to be in the office. I wanted to be standing in front of a boardroom full of people calling the shots, but since I'd crashed into Bella, the only place I seemed to want to be was by her side.

"Let's go," I encouraged, holding her by the hips and gently pushing her away from me, instantly missing her warmth.

After helping her down into the gondola, I climbed down the ladder and settled beside her. If anyone saw me now they wouldn't believe it. I had a reputation for being a player, one that wasn't entirely undeserved. But here I was. Dressed in a tux, in the early evening climbing into a gondola. If someone had told me this is what I'd be doing tonight I'd think they were on crack, but there was no doubt about it.

Tony, our gondolier, had gone above and beyond. When I'd told my assistant to arrange it, I'd told her to find me the best. The best who would play the part and Tony certainly hadn't disappointed. Wearing his black and white striped shirt, his boater hat with an oversized red bow, and pressed black pants, he pushed off effortlessly and steered us through the maze of canals.

Pulling her phone from her purse, Bella started snapping pictures as we passed by landmarks and gave way to gondolas floating in the opposite direction. When she pointed the camera in my direction, I smiled for the first one and then snatched it from her hands.

"Hey!" she protested as I pulled her back to my side. "I was catching memories with that."

"Why don't you let me take them for you, Bella? That way you can be a part of those memories?" I offered, and a thoughtful confusion wrinkled her brow.

When she pouted, I lifted her phone and snapped a selfie of us just as Tony started singing. His deep baritone belted out the lyrics of Dean Martin's classic, 'That's Amore' much to Bella's delight, and soon enough, her frown was turned upside down, and she was smiling and singing along under her breath. She didn't know the words but that didn't seem to faze her. Snapping another picture, this time as I pressed my lips to her temple. I knew I'd never forget this moment and I didn't want her to either, and if that meant filling her phone with photos, then that's what I'd do.

"And over here, *Signora,* is the Rialto Bridge," Tony interrupted, pointing out the crowded bridge up ahead. "It's the oldest bridge in Venice built in the sixteenth century," he added, taking the role of the tour guide. A role I was supposed to be fulfilling, but I was too enamored by the woman in my arms to be remembering historical facts and pointing out things of interest.

"What are all those people doing?" Bella asked, her voice laced with intrigue.

"They're putting a lock on the bridge," I explained.

"You mean people really do that?"

"They do," I confirmed.

"I thought that was just something I saw in movies."

"Not at all. People travel from all over the world to put their locks on the Rialto Bridge symbolizing their indestructible bond and forever love."

"That's beautiful," Bella mused wistfully.

I'd always thought it was corny and trashy and a waste of city resources cutting them off and disposing of them but seeing the hearts in Bella's eyes had me reconsidering my stance. Something I seemed to be doing a lot of in the past twenty-four hours.

Snuggling together as the sun set, we snaked our way through the canals in silence, Bella looking at the world around her, me staring at her. She had no idea how beautiful she really was, inside and out. As we passed under a bridge, I couldn't take it any longer. Leaning over, I caught Bella off-guard when I cupped her face in my hands and kissed her.

It took barely a breath for her to realize what was happening, then her hands were resting over mine, and she was kissing me back just as enthusiastically. When the tiniest of moans escaped her, I seized the opportunity to plunge my tongue in and taste her, something I'd been dying to do all day. Our kiss, which started off sweet and slow, turned to one filled with want and passion and by the time we broke apart, Bella's eyes had darkened, filled with lust reflecting everything I felt.

Resting my forehead against hers, I sucked in deep breaths, not wanting to let her go. "Bella," I breathed.

"Matteo," she replied breathlessly.

Forcing myself to think about anything other than the pulsating need building in my balls, I adjusted her in my arms, holding her close.

We finished our ride in silence, but before I let her out of the gondola, I pulled her in for one last kiss, handing my phone to Tony to capture the moment. Turns out Bella wasn't the only one who wanted to make memories.

Walking back to the car, arm in arm, we looked like all the other couples around us. Perhaps overdressed but glowing in our own little bubble. One I wasn't ready to burst. We went to dinner, and I barely tasted my food. I spent the whole time staring at the woman across the candlelit table wondering how quickly I could strip her out of that decadent red dress and have her writhing beneath me.

"Thank you, Matteo," Bella started as her dessert was set down in front of her. Something she swore she couldn't possibly fit in, but I couldn't not order for her. The moment she'd found it on the menu, I knew it was something she wanted, and that's what I was here for. To give her everything her heart desired. To make all her dreams come true. To give her all the memories she was desperate to make.

"For what, beautiful?"

"Everything. This." She pointed at the cold ricotta cream with pistachio crumble, candied orange, and chocolate in front of her. "For today. For the gondola ride. For all of it. You've made this trip everything I wanted it to be and so much more."

"Bella," I began, taking hold of her hand. "Firstly, you're welcome."

"And second?" she probed, setting down her spoon and holding my hand to hers.

"And second, we're only just getting started."

Chapter Five

Bella

He kissed me.
    Matteo kissed me.

My first real kiss.

A kiss that even now, as I lay in bed, replaying it over and over and over again, I'm barely able to believe really happened.

It was almost midnight, and there was no chance of me falling asleep anytime soon. I was too wired.

I don't think Matteo realizes what he gave to me today. He made my dream come true, showing me around Venice. His patience while I oohed and aahed over practically everything. The way he took the time to explain things or point out things he thought I might like. All the ways he found to touch me, whether it was his hand resting on the small of my back or his fingers tangled with mine. Everything had been perfect. Then he'd gone and topped it off with that kiss. A kiss I wouldn't mind a replay of right now.

But I needed sleep. He was picking me up again in the morning. This time he'd told me where we were headed and what to wear. So, with images of an Italian man with piercing blue eyes, a gold Rolex wrapped around his wrist wearing a tuxedo like it was made for him, I drifted off to sleep with a smile on my face.

The next day was just as incredible. Matteo showed up in jeans and a long-sleeve Henley on the back of that red scooter, and I was done for. He took me into Saint Mark's Basilica before he whipped me over to San Giorgio Maggiore Island, something I didn't even know existed. Turns out having a local show you around Venice got you more than the dollar store guidebook had to offer. Climbing the bell tower gave me a view I never wanted to look away from.

But as incredible as the day was, as amazing as the architecture was, as beautiful as the old artworks that lined the walls of the churches were, nothing could compare to the man beside me. He had me completely bewitched.

Then, as if he hadn't already done enough for me, Matteo took me to a late lunch.

"Where's the menu?" I asked in a hushed tone, not wanting to look stupid. I felt underdressed as it was in my cream linen pants and burgundy tank.

"There isn't one, *mi amore*."

"Then how do I know what to order?"

"Trust me," Matteo asked.

And there he went again. Trust me. Every time he said it, I got goosebumps yet every time I gave in and let him take the lead. So far, I had no regrets.

A moment later, a server appeared carrying our first course. I didn't know what, but it was as impressive as those artworks I'd been admiring all day.

"Where are we?" I whispered, looking around, finding we were all alone.

"We, *tesoro,* are at a restaurant called Oro. They customize the menu for us based on what we tell them."

"And what did we tell them?" I enquired, fascinated by the idea.

"We told them that it was our first time in Venice, our first time in Italy and we wanted to experience only the very best they had to offer."

"We told them all that, did we?" I asked, taking a sip of my mineral water which had also magically appeared.

"We did."

"And did we happen to also tell them that we were contagious or something? Where are the other diners?"

"They only offer seating for five tables. We just happened to have mentioned, that we'd prefer that number to be only one," Matteo confirmed, looking rather pleased with himself.

"Matteo…" This man. He'd gone so far above and beyond there was no way I could ever repay him. "Thank you."

"You're welcome, Bella."

We had the most incredible meal. Everything was so fresh and delicious, by the time we were leaving, I wondered how much it cost to have a personal chef on standby every day. Definitely more than a pharmacist earns that was for sure.

Standing on the dock, waiting for our boat to pick us up and take us back to the main island, I looked up at Matteo, his eyes hidden behind his aviators, and I couldn't not kiss him. I'd never kissed a man before, especially one like Matteo, but I wanted to. Desperately. Yesterday when he'd kissed me, I'd been caught off-guard, but today I wanted to be the one to initiate it.

All day I'd been waiting for him to do it again. I wanted to feel his lips pressed against mine, but other than the few light pecks on my cheek and forehead, he hadn't even tried.

"Matteo?"

"Yes, Bella?" he replied, turning to face me.

Taking the opportunity, I pressed up on my toes, put my hands on his shoulder to keep me from toppling over, and pressed my lips against his. Reacting on instinct, Matteo's arms wound around my waist, crushing me to him as he took control, his tongue plunging into my mouth.

Someone clearing their throat behind us brought us back to reality. A reality I didn't want to come back to. Being wrapped up in Matteo was heaven and the only place I wanted to be.

"*Signore, la tua barca,*" he said apologetically, indicating the waiting boat bobbing on the water.

"Let's go."

Matteo helped me down into the boat before sitting beside me and pulling me into his lap. As the boat bounced across the waves, Matteo kissed me like a man possessed. Beneath my butt I could feel the hard ridge of his dick. I might be an inexperienced virgin, but it was undeniable.

We reached the car before we knew it and Matteo helped me up the ladder. Shock flickered through my body when his hand landed on my ass, but I didn't hate it. Sliding into the backseat, I practically scrambled into his lap. I had no idea what I was doing, but if Matteo noticed, he didn't seem to mind.

"Bella," he groaned as he kissed my throat, a kiss that I felt *everywhere.*

"*Signore?*" his driver interrupted, and I glanced out the window to find we were already idling out the front of the hotel.

With one last kiss, Matteo pulled away, and instantly I felt cold. I didn't want to let him go. Forty-eight hours and the man was under my skin. I'd dated David for almost three months, and I hadn't once wanted him as badly as I wanted Matteo. He hadn't made me feel half the things Matteo did.

"Come upstairs with me," I practically begged, not even ashamed.

"Bella?" My name was a question. He wanted reassurance, and I wanted him.

"Come upstairs with me, Matteo," I repeated more confidently this time.

"I was going to take you out for dinner," he replied, still unsure.

"We can order room service," I replied, sounding like I knew what I was doing when the truth was, I was winging it.

Rattling off something in Italian to his driver, Matteo helped me from the car and then took my hand leading me up the steps and into the lobby. Arriving at the elevator, he pressed the call button and we waited in silence, shoulder to shoulder. Anxiety was creeping in about what I was about to do. Anxiety, not regret.

Stepping into the elevator, the mirrored doors closed, and Matteo was on me. Gone was the gentleman he'd been all day, he was lost in a fog and all he could see was me. When he grabbed my ass and lifted me, my legs wrapped around his waist on instinct. Hormones were running this show, no doubt about it. Grinding against him, I buried my hands in his hair tugging harshly as he kissed me ferociously.

The bell dinged, and we arrived on my floor. Matteo slid me down his body, the thick, hard ridge of his cock prominent in his jeans. Grabbing my hand, he dragged me into the corridor.

"Which way, Bella?"

Pointing to my room, I dug the key from my purse.

Reaching the door, Matteo pinned me against it, not caring who was around or where we were. His hands were everywhere. In my hair. Trailing down over my ribs. Squeezing my hips. While I tried to force the key in the lock, Matteo purred against my neck making every hair on my body stand on end.

"Finally," I heaved, managing to get the key in and the door open.

Falling through the door, I dropped my bag where it fell completely ignorant of everything but the man in front of me as he untucked my top.

Ignoring the trembling in my fingers, I helped Matteo out of his shirt, and my jaw nearly hit the floor. I knew he was all muscle beneath the material, but knowing it and seeing it were two completely different things. He was tanned and lean and had the most mind-scrambling V I'd ever seen. He was a work of art, putting all others I'd seen today to shame.

"You have too many clothes on, *amore mio,*" Matteo cooed, reaching for the hem of my top and dragging it over my head.

Tossing it behind him, Matteo growled, his eyes fixed on my heaving chest, and I was sure I would self-combust. I might've been a virgin, but I was also a thirty-two-year-old woman who'd been taking care of myself for a long time. The heated look on Matteo's face, the way he licked his lips, the way he trailed his fingertip across the top of my black lace bra had me already well aware that everything that had ever come before him was going to pale in comparison.

When I was stripped down to my underwear, Matteo prowled toward me. Taking a step back I stumbled, landing on the bed, Matteo staring down at me. I should've been afraid. Anxious. Scared even. The only thing coursing through my veins right now was desperate need and want.

"*Sei bello,*" he mumbled. And although I didn't have a clue what he said, it didn't matter.

Reaching for his belt, he batted my hands away. "Not yet. First, I feast," he said, and I dropped my head back against the mattress as Matteo fell to his knees, nudging mine open and wedging his shoulders between them.

As he trailed open mouth kisses along the inside of my thigh I shivered, barely able to believe this was really happening. Matteo was going to be my first. My first everything and I was so glad I waited.

When I felt the warmth of his breath where I needed him the most, his fingers reached up pushing aside the lace of my panties as if they were offensive, before groaning loudly. "*Bellissima,*" he groaned, leaning forward and taking a deep breath.

At the first lap of his tongue, I almost shot off the bed. "Wait!"

Chapter Six
Matteo

"Wait!" Bella cried out, and I froze. This had never happened to me before. Here I was about to devour her like a starving man, something that describes me perfectly and she was calling a halt to it.

Swallowing down my emotions, I focused on the beautiful woman splayed out in front of me. Black lace has never looked so good. Her pointed nipples tried to break free of their lace cage as her chest heaved. Her cheeks had turned a deep shade of red, and the scent of her arousal was thick in the air.

"What is it, *amore mio?*"

"I...I..."

"You what, Bella," I encouraged softly.

"I've-never-done-this-before," she rushed out, looking away and trying to squeeze her legs shut. At least that's what I thought I heard.

"You've never done what before?" I tried to confirm only for her to throw her arm over her face as she attempted to hide from me.

"This. All of it."

Lifting myself off the floor, I took her arm and pulled it away from her face. "Beautiful, Bella. Are you telling me you've never had the pleasure of having a man eat your pretty pussy?" I asked, watching as she winced at my crassness. "Or are you telling me you've never had a man..." I stalled. The word fuck was on the tip of my tongue, but the truth was I didn't want to fuck Bella. I knew I wouldn't be able to. She wasn't like that, and if we only had a short time, then I needed to make it count. Leave her with a memory she'd never forget. Instead, I asked, "You've never had a man make love to you before?"

Bella groaned and tried to roll away, but there was no way I was letting her escape. I was already trying to find ways to keep her, knowing she was untouched made her mine.

"Bella, talk to me."

"Fine. Neither. I'm a pathetic thirty-two-year-old virgin," Bella spat like it tasted bitter on her tongue. When I didn't flinch, even managing to keep the cocky grin that was bubbling inside me from escaping, she pushed. "Don't you want to run away now? Don't you think something is wrong with me?"

"*Mio Caro,* there's absolutely nothing wrong with you. And I'm not going anywhere. But I am going to take my time and make this special for you," I promised, ignoring my throbbing cock which was straining my jeans.

"Matteo..." My name fell like a plea from Bella's lips, and I leaned down and kissed away her fears. I wasn't going anywhere without her. Not this minute. Not today. And if I could find a way, not ever.

I made love to Bella, committing every moan, every groan, every movement her body made to memory. Then over the next three days, between excursions out sightseeing and meals shared in cozy restaurants, we spent hours tangled in the sheet of her hotel room making memories neither of us would ever forget.

Chapter Seven
Bella

Today was the day I had to go home.

I didn't want to go.

I wanted to crawl back into bed, snuggle up in Matteo's arms, and pretend the real world didn't exist. Except it did. And it was time for me to get back to it.

Staring at the woman in the mirror, I barely recognized her. She looked happy. Content. At peace with the world around her. And for the first time, that's how I felt. I don't know if it was all the beauty I'd seen, the amazing food I'd overindulged in or the man still snoring in our sex-stained sheets, but I was for the first time that I could remember truly happy.

"*Buongiorno, amore mio,*" Matteo greeted, sneaking up behind me and nuzzling my neck.

"Good morning," I replied, smiling like a loon in love.

"I want to take you somewhere before your flight," he announced.

"You don't have to do that. I can get a taxi..."

"Bella. Please. Let me do this," he asked sincerely, and I couldn't say no to him. I doubted I ever could. Thankfully, he hadn't asked me to stay because there were things I hadn't told him, things I couldn't explain, and if I stayed, there was no way I'd be able to avoid the truth.

"Okay," I agreed, kissing his cheek.

After a shared shower, one designed to save water but we ended up staying in there until the water ran cool, we dressed, and I packed my things. After double-checking I had everything, Matteo picked up my suitcase, took my hand, and we left our bubble.

Sitting in the back of Matteo's car, I stared out the window, drinking everything in one last time. The man sitting beside me, with stubble on his jaw, ran his thumb back and forth over my hand he was holding in his lap.

When we pulled to a stop, Matteo ushered me out of the car, pausing to speak to his driver before leading me around the corner. We were standing at the Rialto Bridge. Already people were gathered everywhere, and when Matteo pulled a padlock from his pocket, I almost cried. How was I ever going to get over this man?

"This is so we never forget, *amore mio*."

"Matteo." My heart was so full I thought it was going to burst. "How could I ever forget?"

Placing the lock in my hand, I turned it over, and engraved in a beautiful old-fashioned script were our names.

Matteo & Bella ~ forever

Tears filled my eyes as Matteo led me through the people before kneeling down and taking the lock from me. When he added it to the fence, rising back to his feet, he kissed me like it was the last time and all I could hope was that it wasn't.

I wasn't ready to let him go.

I didn't want to let him go.

"Come," he gestured, leading me back to the car.

The whole trip to the airport, I sobbed in Matteo's arms. How was this fair? I'd only just found him, and now I had to say goodbye.

After I checked in, we sat in silence waiting for my flight to be called and when it was, my heart shattered.

"Thank you, Bella. I've had an incredible time with you," Matteo started, and I cried harder. Ugly tears blurred my vision and I sniffed loudly. "Please don't cry, *amore mio.*"

"I'm sorry," I sobbed.

"You have nothing to be sorry for, my beautiful Bella. I love you," he said, and my head snapped up.

"You do?"

"I do. With everything I am, I love you, *amore mio,*" Matteo offered, wiping my tears away with his thumb before kissing my lips so tenderly.

"I love you too. I know it's fast and I know we don't know everything there is to know about each other. And we live a million miles apart, but I love you too, Matteo. And I don't want to go. We'll never see each other again."

With a wide smile, one filled with love and something more. Something I'd seen before. "Oh, my beautiful Bella. Where there's a will, there's a way. Trust me."

The End...
Or is it, only the beginning?

What Next?

Can't get enough of Bella and Matteo's love story?
Need to know if their love is strong enough to endure the tests of time,
difference, family commitments?

***

MATTEO IS LIVE NOW!

***

Matteo

My time with Bella McIntosh was only supposed to last a week—I needed to focus on the family business—but I'd soon realize I couldn't let her go.

She haunted my dreams and drove me to the point of distraction.

That's how I found myself on the verge of saying 'I do', but deep down, I knew I couldn't go through with it.

Leaving my bride at the altar wasn't part of the plan, but I had to follow my heart ... which was on the other side of the world.

I could only hope she'd never forget the time we shared.

Bella

I had everything I ever wanted ... except him.

Matteo Mancini.

He was supposed to be a vacation fling, but he turned out to be so much more.

We promised each other forever, but our time ended before we got that chance.

I left my heart in Italy and returned home to focus on the life I was building. All the while pretending I was over him, but I wasn't. I never would be.

We lived a world apart ... if only our love was strong enough to withstand the obstacles that stood in our way.

Also By

Standalones

One Night Only

Rise Up

Broken Promises

Shattered Dreams

Fallen

Playing Games Series

Marked

Played

Benched

Playing the Field Series

Overtime

Rookie

Offside
Taking the Court

Rebound

Slam Dunk

Home Court
Finding Your Place Series

Coming Home

Running Away

Believing Again
Meet the McIntyres Series

Taking Charge

Picturing Perfect

Fighting Back

Breaking Free

Finding Forever

A Merry McIntyre Christmas

Meet the McIntyres Boxset
Second Chance Series

Second Chance Forever

Second Chance Heart

Second Chance Family
Billionaires

Matteo

Dante

Hudson

Acknowledgements

This one is short and sweet and allowed me to step out of my comfort zone and try something new. To say I fell in love with the smooth, sophisticated Italian is an understatement.

Thank you for reading Bella's love story. Thank you for taking the chance. Your support enables me to keep following my dreams and let's be honest, who knows where we'll end up, but with your support, I know it will be worth the adventure.

As always I can't say enough nice things and show how much I've come to love, adore and appreciate the dream team who stand beside me each and every time. Kath, Marg, Marns, Dana... you ladies make this ride worth every minute. Thank you for being my circle!

Some people are lucky enough to find their person, but I got my very own book boyfriend. He might not be Italian. He might not be a billionaire with his own private jet. He might not even have the perfect six pack abs or the 'V' that makes smart girls dumb, but he's my person. Rob, I couldn't imagine any one else I'd want to spend Friday nights, sitting on the couch in our sweatpants eating takeout and watching the football with. Thank you for always supporting me in everything I do.

So, until next time...

Love Rebecca

xoxo

About the Author

Rebecca lives in Australia's capital surrounded by bushland and kangaroos. When she's not writing about small town romance or sexy athletes she's watching football with her husband, snuggling up with their dog or indulging in some very yummy chocolates.

Stay Connected

Website: www.rebeccabarberauthor.com
Facebook Page: Barber's Bellas
Instagram: @RebeccaBarber7
Twitter: @RebeccaBarber7

Made in the USA
Columbia, SC
03 June 2024